MOOSE
AT
WORK

DUCK DUCK MOOSE

Dave Horowitz

G. P. Putnam's Sons Penguin Young Readers Group

One day in the Great North Woods ...

"Sure is getting cold," said Duck.

"I'm f-f-freezing," said Other Duck.

"Just the way I like it," said Moose.

"We're going *south* for the winter," said Other Duck.

"No way," said Moose. "I like it right here.
Bear will get pancakes with me."

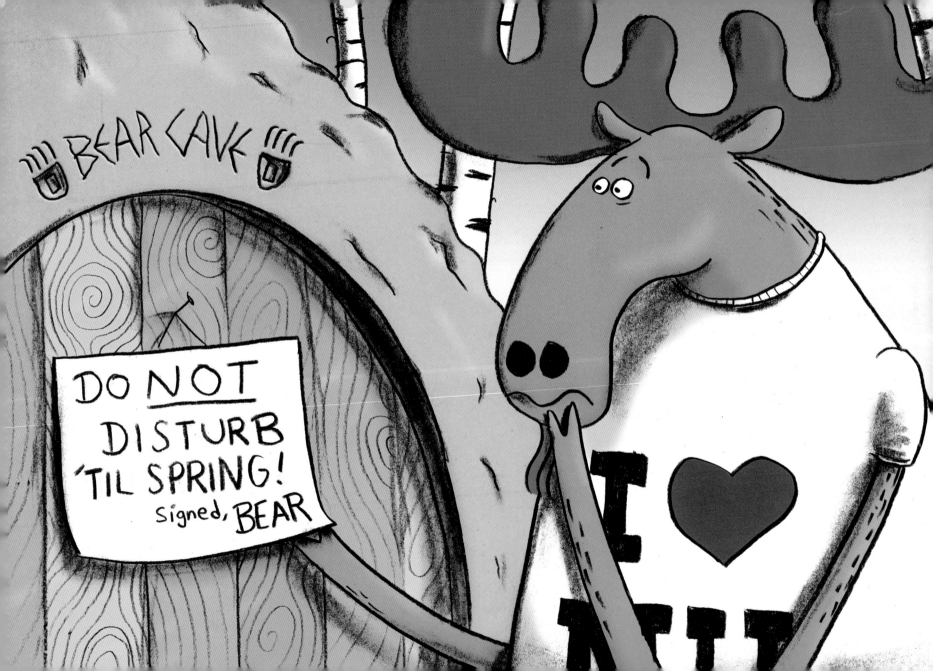

But Bear was already hibernating.

"You've got to be kidding," said Moose.

"I guess I'll have to go and get pancakes
by myself."

But the Pancake Hut was closed until spring.

This is going to be one long and lonely winter, thought Moose.

Unless...

"Hey," said Other Duck.
"I see Washington, D.C.!"

"Hey!" said Moose.
"I've got to pee!"

Somewhere in Georgia, the friends got stuck in a traffic jam.

"Row, row, row yer boat," sang Duck.

"Gently down the stream," sang Other Duck.

"Oh, brother," said Moose.

"Look," said Duck. "A shell."

"Look," said Other Duck. "A starfish."

"Look," said Moose. "A sea monster!"

Next stop, Larry's U-pik.

"I picked an orange," said Duck.

"I picked a grapefruit," said Other Duck.

"I pick me!" said Moose.

And the fun went on

...and on ...and on.

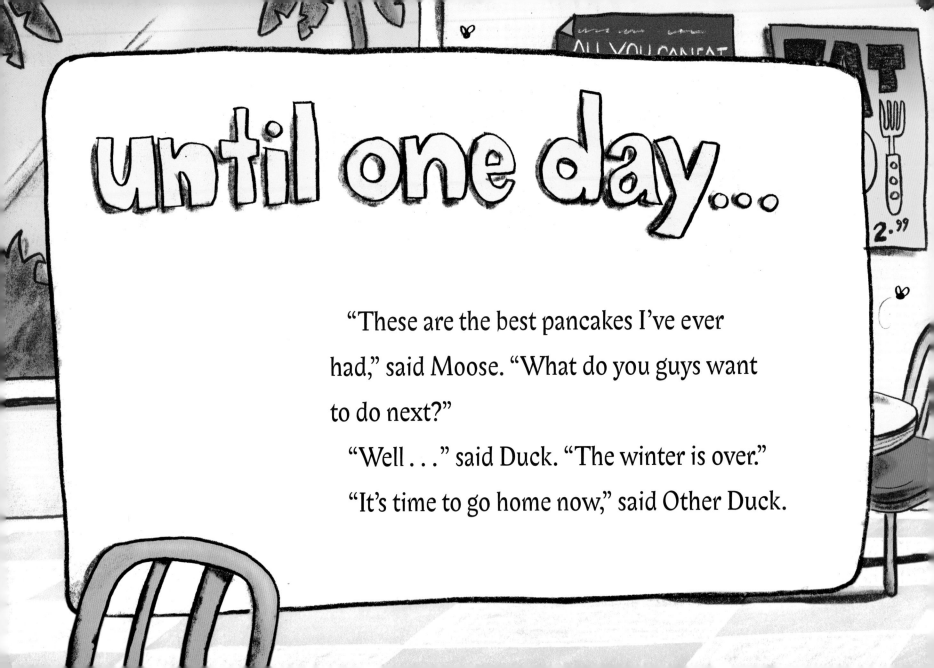

until one day...

"These are the best pancakes I've ever had," said Moose. "What do you guys want to do next?"

"Well . . ." said Duck. "The winter is over."

"It's time to go home now," said Other Duck.

"Sure is good to be back," said Duck.

"It's getting kind of warm," said Other Duck.

"Just the way I like it!" said Moose.

THE END

FOR
JUSTIN FERREN
AND
TYLOR DURAND.

Author's Note: All characters and events in this book are fictional. Any resemblance to the family road trips the author was forced to go on as a child is purely coincidental—especially page 17!

Acknowledgments: As always, the author thanks Nancy Paulsen, Cecilia Yung, Richard Amari and Sara Kreger, the finest art and editorial team this side of the Mason-Dixon line.

G. P. PUTNAM'S SONS
A division of Penguin Young Readers Group.
Published by The Penguin Group. Penguin Group (USA) Inc., 375 Hudson Street, New York, NY 10014, U.S.A. Penguin Group (Canada), 90 Eglinton Avenue East, Suite 700, Toronto, Ontario M4P 2Y3, Canada (a division of Pearson Penguin Canada Inc.). Penguin Books Ltd, 80 Strand, London WC2R 0RL, England. Penguin Ireland, 25 St. Stephen's Green, Dublin 2, Ireland (a division of Penguin Books Ltd.). Penguin Group (Australia), 250 Camberwell Road, Camberwell, Victoria 3124, Australia (a division of Pearson Australia Group Pty Ltd). Penguin Books India Pvt Ltd, 11 Community Centre, Panchsheel Park, New Delhi - 110 017, India. Penguin Group (NZ), 67 Apollo Drive, Rosedale, North Shore 0632, New Zealand (a division of Pearson New Zealand Ltd). Penguin Books (South Africa) (Pty) Ltd, 24 Sturdee Avenue, Rosebank, Johannesburg 2196, South Africa. Penguin Books Ltd, Registered Offices: 80 Strand, London WC2R 0RL, England.

Manufactured in China by South China Printing Co. Ltd.
Design by Richard Amari. Text set in Biblon.
The art was done with black pencil and charcoal on newsprint. Color was added digitally.
Library of Congress Cataloging-in-Publication Data
Horowitz, Dave, 1970– Duck, duck, moose / Dave Horowitz. p. cm. Summary: With no prospect of any friends around for the winter, Moose decides to travel south with Duck and Other Duck. [1. Moose—Fiction. 2. Ducks—Fiction. 3. Travel—Fiction.] I. Title. PZ7.H78755Du 2009 [E]—dc22 2008053357.
ISBN 978-0-399-24782-8
1 3 5 7 9 10 8 6 4 2